*Samuel French Acting Edition*

# Beneath the Surface

*Book by*
Don & Lynn Stallings

*Music & Lyrics by*
Erik Grant Bennett

*Additional Rap Lyrics by*
Tyrone Houston

SAMUELFRENCH.COM    SAMUELFRENCH.CO.UK

BENEATH THE SURFACE was originally produced by THE ATLANTA WORKSHOP PLAYERS. The production was Directed by Lynn Stallings, with Musical Direction by Erik Grant Bennett, and was Choreographed by KC Powe Bennett, with the following cast:

| | | |
|---|---|---|
| TEACHER | Bree Shannon | |
| | Don Stallings | J.T. Alessi |
| SWINGS | Amber Brooke | Johanna Braddy |
| | Tiffany Clark | |
| ANGEL | Chiwuzo (Ife) Okwumabua | Teka Matthews |
| DEREK | Rico Sisney | Brandon Chubbs |
| JAKE | Wesley Jetton | Taylor Darden |
| JANE | Greyson Chadwick | Mallory Tarter |
| LUKE | Garland Hunt | Brandon Jenkins |
| SKYE | Jennifer Jacoby | Katie Scott Sisterhen |
| | Grace Freeman | |

# CHARACTERS

**JAKE** — Is a star football player whose life-long dream of going to college on a sports scholarship and playing professional ball is shattered with a serious knee injury. He is now struggling to redefine himself & find a new direction for his life.

**DEREK** — is a brilliant student who has gotten caught up in a street gang. He wants to get out. He wants a future but he feels trapped. He is on a self-destructive path.

**AMY**— is the all-American, popular, over-achiever. Excellent grades, cheerleader, Vice President of the Senior class, drama club etc. She's typically happy and grounded, but has allowed herself to give into extreme pressure from her boyfriend and now she's pregnant.

**ANGEL**— Is dealing with a harsh home-life. Everyone assumes she is heavy into drugs because of the way she dresses and her angry, distant attitude. In reality, it's her parents who have the substance abuse problem and she has to take on the role of caretaker for her little sister & her parents. She has never known parental love and affection. Now it's up to her to break the chain.

**LUKE**— is a guy with a passionate desire to reach out to the less fortunate in the world. His life plan is to travel to third world countries to help ease the suffering. He will probably start by joining the Peace Corps. His parents are very successful professionals who wish a more traditional path for their son. They love him dearly, but do not support his passion.

**SKYE**— has kept a devastating secret since she was a small child. She has been living in fear and humiliation as the victim of abuse in her own household. When this information surfaces the shock turns to action as the others help Skye make plans to tell the authorities.

**JANE**— is grounded, happy, together, content. She and her family have a great relationship. Sometimes the kids tease her about being so happy & get irritated with what they think is a perfect life. She does have challenges in life, like all people do. She just chooses to dwell on the good things.

**TEACHER**— (Could be male or female) is cool and determined to make a difference in the student's lives.  She has experienced many of the same challenges these kids are facing in her own life. Sometimes it seems as though there is no way to get through to them, but she keeps trying because she realizes that they are worth it.

# MUSICAL NUMBERS

*" Can U Dig It"*.................................................................Company
*" My Reality"*.......................................................................Angel
*" So Much More"*....................................................Jake & Company
*" Communication Breakdown"*.................................................Company
*" Bleeding Heart"*.....................................................Luke & Company
*" Stop"*............................................................Teacher & Company
*" Stop Reprise"*.....................................................Teacher & Company
*" What I See"*.........................................................Derek & Teacher
*" Plain Jane"*.........................................................Jane & Company
*" Can U Dig It?"*.................................................................Company

**#1 Sound Cue: *"Can U Dig It?"***

*(The characters begin in the audience. They stand as they sing.)*

**LUKE.**
STAND UP WHEN U FEEL THE POWER (REPEAT 3 TIMES)

**JAKE.**
STAND UP WHEN U FEEL THE POWER (REPEAT 2 TIMES)

**JANE.**
STAND UP WHEN U FEEL THE POWER

**ALL.**
STAND UP; CAN U FEEL THE POWER (NOW?)

**GUYS.**
CAN U DIG IT?  CAN U DIG IT?
CAN U DIG IT?  CAN U DIG IT?
(CAN U DIG IT, COME ON) *(Woah...)*

**ALL.**
CAN U DIG IT?  CAN U DIG IT? (What, (repeats 6 times) hey...)
CAN U DIG IT?  CAN U DIG IT?
(CAN U DIG IT)

**DEREK.**
LOOK AROUND, YO….AIN'T LIKE IT'S BRAIN SURGERY
CAN'T U SEE THAT YOU AND ME IS THE SAME?
SO WHAT WE LIVE A LITTLE DIFFERENTLY?
WE DISAGREE, BUT WE STILL BELIEVE
WHEN YA BREAK IT DOWN, THERE'S ALWAYS COMMON
     GROUND
THOUGH THE SURFACE AT FIRST CAN APPEAR 2 BE SHAL-
     LOW,
IT'S WORTH A SECOND LOOK CUZ U MISTOOK THE FIRST
     TIME AROUND
BENEATH THE SURFACE, IT'S DEEP ENOUGH 2 DROWN-
     TELL ME….

**ALL.**
CAN U DIG IT?  CAN U DIG IT?
CAN U DIG IT?  CAN U DIG IT?
(CAN U DIG IT, COME ON)
CAN U DIG IT?  CAN U DIG IT?
CAN U DIG IT?  CAN U DIG IT?
(CAN U DIG IT)

**DEREK.**
*(Sung during above section.)*

LEMME SEE YA JUMP, JUMP, JUMP
JUMP, JUMP, JUMP, HEY…
PUT YOUR HANDS UP, PUT YOUR HANDS UP
PUT YOUR HANDS UP – LEMME HEAR YA SAY…
HOO, HOO….LEMME HEAR YA SAY HOO HOO
ONE MORE TIME, HOO HOO….THAT'S RIGHT
LISTEN UP; LISTEN UP; LISTEN UP….

**GUYS.**
DON'T FIGHT IT, CAN'T DENY IT
MIGHT BE SURPRISED IF U TRY IT
SOME HIDE IT, GET SHORT-SIGHTED

**DEREK.**
U SELLIN' HATE?  DON'T TRIP?  (ANGEL.  I WON'T BUY IT)
WE CAN SPREAD THE CURE, NOT THE DISEASE
WE GOT 2 RELEASE ALL THE FEAR AND ADHERE 2 OUR
    OWN BELIEFS

**JANE.**
THERE'S MORE 2 ME THAN WHAT U SEE.

**ALL.**
DITCH THE LABELS AND….

**GUYS.**
SET YOUR MIND FREE!

**ALL.**
WUZ UP (WUZ UP)
WUZ UP (WUZ UP)
WUZ UP (WUZ UP)
WUZ UP (WUZ UP)
WUZ UP (WUZ UP)
WUZ UP (WUZ UP)
WUZ UP

**DEREK.** Now sing.

**ALL.**
CAN U DIG IT?  CAN U DIG IT?
CAN U DIG IT?  CAN U DIG IT?
(CAN U DIG IT, COME ON)
CAN U DIG IT?  CAN U DIG IT?
CAN U DIG IT?  CAN U DIG IT?
(CAN U DIG IT)

**DEREK.**
*(Sung during above section.)*

HERE WE GO NOW; HERE WE GO NOW
HERE WE GO NOW; HERE WE GO, COME ON
YEAH, YEAH, YEAH, YEAH, YEAH, YEAH, WOAH…

HERE WE GO...
Y'ALL FEEL THAT?

*(All freeze in a happy, connected tableau.)*

**TEACHER.** *(ENTERS and speaks to audience, referring to students in the frozen, happy tableau.)* Take a look at this....on the surface, 7 very different teenagers....so what's wrong with this picture? *(Laughs)* Nothing. *(Students break freeze & laugh playfully.)* but *(Students freeze again.)* 48 hours ago...now that's a different story. Let's go back and look. *(Students find themselves in a classroom. They peal off with cold, angry attitudes, glaring at each other, avoiding each other & go to chairs to sit as they say these lines.)*

**JAKE..** I can't believe I'm missing the Tech game to be here!

**ANGEL..** *(Angry as she goes to sit down in a corner on the floor --- just wants people out of her way.)* Back off.

**SKYE.** As bad as this sucks, it sure beats being at home.

**DEREK..** *(Yawning)* What's this about anyway?

**LUKE.** Is it a test?

**JANE.** *(Pleasantly)* I guess we'll see!

**AMY.** I've got enough on my mind already.

**TEACHER.** Good morning class. Do you know why you're here on this fine Saturday morning?

**JAKE.** You're mad at us?

**ANGEL.** *(Lifting head off desk.)* Because we've angered the Gods and this is our punishment?

**SKYE.** *(Sarcastic, in mock cheerleader style.)* I thought this was the pep rally.

**TEACHER.** No...you're here because you haven't completed your Senior Community Service project.

**DEREK.** Yeah....I was uh meanin' to talk to you 'bout that.

**JAKE.** Hey, I've been in rehab.

**ALL.** *(All look surprised)* Rehab?

**JAKE.** For my knee people! For my knee.

**SKYE.** Yeah, whatever.

**LUKE.** I think the whole idea of the school coercing us, nay....extorting work from us to help the community reeks of forced socialism.

**ALL KIDS.** *(Agreeing w/the hope of getting out of doing the project.)* Yeah!

**TEACHER.** Did I mention you must complete this senior project to graduate?

**LUKE.** Did I mention it sounds like a great opportunity to help people? *(Sincere)* For real, I mean it.

**TEACHER.** Well, that's more like it. And, since you have all neglected to choose a project, I have one for you.

**STUDENTS.** *(Ad-libs.)* Aw, man. Wait a minute. Shouldn't we have a say in this?...etc.

**SKYE.** Hey, my idea is to solve two social dilemmas at once.

**TEACHER.** Oh, really?

**SKYE.** *(Making a big deal about this 'great' idea. Others intently listening.)* Yeah, picture this...' <u>FEED</u> the homeless...<u>TO</u>...the hungry.

**ALL KIDS.** *(Reacting with shock, disgust etc.)* Aw, man! Whoa.

**AMY.** That's disgusting.

**SKYE.** Well, we'd cook them first.

*(This causes big reactions and a flurry of people trying to get SKYE to hush & sit down.)*

**AMY.** And that makes it better how?

**SKYE.** You could use BBQ sauce.

**ALL.** *(Stopping SKYE.)* Hey!

**TEACHER.** *(Ill at ease.)* Okay. *(Changing subject.)* Now, your project is based on the fact that once you were all best friends, but you've chosen different paths. It's called "Project Reconnect" to help show that we can bridge our differences. You'll share what you discover to help stop friction in the school. Your presentation to the entire student body will be in an assembly on Monday.

**ALL..** *(Most jump up loudly protesting to the TEACHER. JANE tries to rally people together. ANGEL sits in chair, angry etc. Ad libs.)* What? No way. It's too soon. Monday? You're kidding, right? Forget it! I'm out!

**TEACHER.** This is a group project. *Everyone* is involved or no one passes.

*(Various reactions from; "cool" to "this is so lame" etc. TEACHER steps away and breaks the fourth wall, addressing the audience — the group freezes.)*

**TEACHER.** Well, that was one hour ago...let's see how they're doing. *(TEACHER steps back into scene — STUDENTS abruptly break out of freeze, arguing heatedly — screaming. There is chaos in the room.)* Hey. *(They get quiet. TEACHER goes to do paper work at her desk upstage left.)* Get to work.

**JANE.** Okay, look guys, we have a chance to create a legacy that will make a difference in this school and the lives of all its students.

**JAKE.** *(Getting back to business.)* I don't get it... "Project Reconnect"?

**ANGEL.** Project Reconnect. What's that mean?

**LUKE.** Well, think about it. Ms. Watson got us together...

**AMY.** ...'cause we used to be friends.

**JAKE.** Yeah, used to be.

**SKYE.** So she wants us to reconnect.

**DEREK.** *(Sarcastic)* Yeah and then share our happy plan and bring peace and harmony to the school.

**AMY.** That would be so cool.

**LUKE.** *(Sincerely)* That would be cool. Okay, think...what do we have in common?

**SKYE.** We have the same number of chromosomes.

**DEREK.** Ms. Watson likes to torture us.

**TEACHER.** *(Looking up from paperwork.)* Ms. Watson can hear you.

**JAKE.** We all hate Brussel sprouts.

**LUKE.** I like them.

**ANGEL.** Luke, you were always the weird one.

**LUKE.** *(Flirting a bit.)* Yeah, but you always liked me best. *(Students react to flirting playfully - LUKE changes subject.)* Okay, when we were kids, we all wanted to be Luke Skywalker, right?

**ANGEL.** I think that was just you.

**TEACHER.** *(Throws LUKE a drumming stick to use as a light saber — playing into the "Star Wars" thing.)* Luke! May the force be with you! *(LUKE catches 'light saber' and 'becomes' Luke

*Skywalker leaping about in a duel with an imaginary opponent.)*

**JAKE.** *(Playing along in best Darth Vader voice)* Luke, I am your father!

*(LUKE ends up on the floor after wild battle with invisible opponent.)*

**SKYE.** Weird.

**ANGEL.** I rest my case. Look, it was easier when we were younger... *(She walks away.)*

**LUKE.** C'mon Angel, we're just trying to figure this out. Open up a little...I know there's more to you than this angry Satanic rock chick.

**ANGEL.** *(Goes over the edge —— walking LUKE back with each word.)* What did you just call me? WHAT DID YOU JUST SAY?! Look, Luke, do not EVER presume to judge me...you don't know me...no one KNOWS me.

**LUKE.** I just said I thought there was more to you, more than you show...

**ANGEL.** *(Interrupting - bitter.)* Oh, yeah, there's more. There's LOTS more.

*(ANGEL looks to TEACHER pleading for help out of this. She starts to walk away.)*

**TEACHER.** *(To LUKE.)* Ask her about her home life.

**LUKE.** Aw c'mon, that's too personal.

**TEACHER.** If you want to get close to some one it's going to get personal...

**LUKE.** But Ms. Watson?

**TEACHER.** ...and when you get closer you might see things that will surprise you...go on, ask her about *her* life. *(LUKE hesitates. TEACHER turns him around & nudges him.)* Go.

**LUKE.** *(Slowly crosses to ANGEL.)* So what's up at home? *(No response.)* What's up at home?

**SKYE.** *(Blurts out.)* Her parents are drunks.

**ANGEL.** *(To SKYE —— furious.)* Shut up.

**SKYE.** Well, they are. They're too wasted to take care of her little sister so she...

**ANGEL.** *(Fiercely)* SHUT-UP!

**LUKE.** That's heavy.

**AMY.** Is that true?

**ANGEL.** *(Angry out burst.)* Yeah, it's true. So what?...*(Long pause.)* I'm the girl who hides her dad's keys 'cause he's too drunk to drive my sister to soccer...I pull the beer cans out of my passed out mother's hand and clean up her empties because *(Glaring at SKYE — angry that she told everyone.)* I don't want my friends to know. I help my little sister with her homework because no one else cares.

**JAKE.** Awww, a druggie with a heart.

**ANGEL.** Druggie? *(Outraged, she runs to attack JAKE. JAKE stumbles over his chair as he tries to get out of her way.)* Back off you stupid jock! *(TEACHER intervenes, physically holding ANGEL back as she continues to go after JAKE.)* Where'd you get that? I've never touched the stuff. I've NEVER touched the stuff. I've seen what it does to people. I live with it.

**JAKE.** *(Genuinely baffled, flustered.)* I just thought. I mean look at you.

**ANGEL.** Look at me? What? You think you can tell who a person is by what they wear? You don't know me — you don't have a clue!

**LUKE.** *(Kindly.)* That's a lot to deal with.

**ANGEL.** *(Still bitter.)* Yeah, so there's more to me!

**SKYE.** *(Trying to lighten the mood.)* Hey, this could be a reality T.V. show.

**ANGEL.** Yeah, but it's not much fun when it's *your* reality.

*(ANGEL'S song- Reveals the pain, anger and loneliness she feels from being neglected by her addicted parents. They depend on her. She longs for their love and stability, but knows it will never come.)*

### #2 Sound Cue: *"MY REALITY"*

**ANGEL.**
I DON'T LIKE TO TALK ABOUT IT – EVERYBODY'S
HEARD THIS STORY – IT'S NO BIG DEAL
*(SPOKEN)* SAME OLD SCHPEAL.
*(Sung)* IT'S JUST MY *LIFE* – WHO REALLY CARES? NOBODY

SAID THE WORLD WAS FAIR, SO LET IT GO.
IT'S JUST ANOTHER DAY – WHAT CAN I SAY?

    **LUKE.** Why do you hide?
    **JAKE.** What's your damage, Angel?
    **ANGEL.** Look, I got dealt a lousy hand…oh well!  Why cry
about it?
    **SKYE.** Maybe you *need* to.
    **LUKE.** Yeah, why act so tough all the time?

    **ANGEL.**
*(Sung)*
CAUSE THIS *IS* MY REALITY – NOT SOME SHOW THAT
    YOU WATCH ON TV
I'M CLEANING UP THE BOTTLES WHEN I SHOULD BE
FAST ASLEEP
BABY, THAT'S MY REALITY

    **AMY.** So your folks are like wasted all the time?
    **ANGEL.** *(Mocking)* Like, yeah.
    **LUKE.** Wow. That's unreal.
    **ANGEL.** Oh no, it's plenty real. I'm seventeen and I feel like
I have to be the parent!
    **DEREK.** That's wack.
    **JANE.**  Come on, girl, let us in.
    **ANGEL.** Alright, Miss "I dot my 'i's with little hearts" — you
asked for it.

*(Sung)*
WHEN I COME HOME MOST EVERY DAY, MY MOM'S
PASSED OUT, TOO DRUNK TO SAY…
"IS THAT MY GIRL?" *(SPOKEN: OR "HOW WAS YOUR DAY?")*
SO I MAKE SOME FOOD, BUT SHE WON'T EAT
THEN DAD COMES HOME AND SHOUTS AT ME
DON'T IT SOUND LIKE FUN?  YEAH, LIFE IS GOOD IN THE
    NEIGHBORHOOD!
I COUNT THE DAYS TILL I CAN LEAVE THIS ALL BEHIND,
    BUT AS FOR NOW, I'LL KEEP ON DOING TIME
CAUSE THIS *IS* MY REALITY – NOT SOME SHOW THAT

YOU WATCH ON TV
I'VE BEEN KNOCKED AROUND SO LONG, I'M USED TO
    MISERY
AND THAT'S JUST MY REALITY

**LUKE.** God, I'm sorry Angel.

**ANGEL.** *(Trying to wipe tears and pretending to be OK.)* Me too. You know…if I had a kid, I'd be so crazy about her. I'd *protect* her and…*(She trails off as she fantasizes.)*

**DEREK.** Well maybe you'll get your chance someday.

**AMY.** Yeah, maybe that's what this is all about — you get to right the wrong, do for your kids what wasn't done for you!

**JANE.** *You* get to break the chain. *You* can decide right now the kind of person you wanna be. Don't let them take that away. *(ANGEL nods in agreement.)*

**ANGEL.**
SO THIS IS MY REALITY – NOT SOME SHOW I JUST
    WATCHED ON TV
BUT I'LL GET THROUGH THE STORM; I KNOW THERE'S
    STILL A CHANCE FOR ME…
CAUSE TIME WILL CHANGE MY REALITY
YES I'LL SURVIVE MY REALITY

**ANGEL.** That is my so-called life!

*(LUKE Smiles — admires her.)*

**ANGEL.** What are you smiling at?

**LUKE.** There is more to you. You're intelligent, compassionate, and if you'd quit wearing that frown, you're kinda pretty *(He smiles again.)*

**ANGEL.** *(Flustered and angry.)* Yeah, well, you know what?

**LUKE.** Yeah, you're wondering what it'd be like to kiss me.

**ANGEL.** *(Hauls off and slaps him.)* That's for assuming I'd want to kiss you! *(Starts to EXIT, pauses then grabs his face & plants a big kiss on him.)* And that's for being right. *(She storms off.)*

**LUKE.** Interesting…

**AMY.** *(Aside to ANGEL.)* I would have been there for you if I'd known.

**ANGEL.** *(Sincere)* Yeah, well, thanks.

**AMY.** I'm here for you now if you need me. *(They hug.)*

*(TEACHER ENTERS & sees hug.)*

**TEACHER.** Well, it looks like at least you two are reconnecting.

**DEREK.** Ms Watson, this is turning into an episode of Dr. Phil.

**SKYE.** *(Teasing him publicly.)* Derek watches Dr. Phil?

**DEREK.** Channel surfing.

**JANE.** *(Sincere)* I like Dr. Phil.

**SKYE.** *(Relentlessly teasing DEREK.)* You like Dr. Phil? *(Laughing)* Derek likes Dr. Phil! Ha!

**DEREK.** *(Very angry — jumps up toward SKYE.)* Ya wanna back off of me nutcase, or we're gonna have a problem.

**TEACHER.** Hey, hey, hey. *(All freeze — teacher addresses the audience.)* This might be a little harder than I thought. *(To students — break freeze.)* Now, get back to work. Just spread out, take a moment and think.

*(All start to scream again — overlapping the following lines.)*

**DEREK.** *(To SKYE.)* What's your problem? Stop. Stop.

**SKYE.** *(To TEACHER.)* It's not my fault. *(Indicating DEREK.)* Talk to him. *(To DEREK.)* You're the problem.

**JANE.** *(To TEACHER.)* We're supposed to work together. I can't do it alone.

**LUKE.** Come on Ms. Watson...what are we supposed to do?

**AMY.** Jane and I are trying...nobody else is trying.

**JAKE.** Ms Watson...Ms Watson...Hey, Ms. Watson.

**ANGEL.** This was a lame idea. What are we doing here?

**TEACHER.** *(Loudly)* Now!

*(They spread out & think quietly. Their personality traits begin to be revealed as they 'wait', 'think'. Someone hiccups. Then another person begins a bored tapping, then add a nervous*

*shift, keep adding sounds until it becomes a friendly challenge and escalates into a fun, step-rhythm piece...an impromptu, percussion, jam session.)*

**JANE.**  See guys, we *can* work together.

**JAKE.** Wishful thinking.  We don't have anything in common anymore.

**JANE.**  Hey, I remember when we were all so tight we were like an odd little family.  We did everything together!  It was like our own version of "Friends".

**LUKE.**  Yeah, good times.....good times.

**ANGEL.** *(To JANE.)* Hey Suzie Cream Cheese, life is not a sit-com.  If it was, I'd hire better writers.

**DEREK.** *(To group.)* Yeah, man...this is wack.  We ain't got nothin' to say to each other.  It's sub-zero between us. *(Referring to AMY.)*  Like, what do I have to say to Miss Cindy Cheerleader here?  She's always gotta be the center of attention.

**AMY.** What?  You don't know anything about me anymore.

**DEREK.** You're right. We don't even speak the same language. *(Starts to EXIT.)*  I'm out.

**AMY.** Wait! Derek....wait. *(He stops & turns.)* So we don't speak the same language. Teach me.

**DEREK.** You dissin me, Yo?

**AMY.** *(Sincerely)*  No. I'm not dish*ing* you. Teach me.

**DEREK.** Aw, that's wack.

**AMY.** *(Still very sincere.)* Like that...teach me that 'wack' thing. I'm serious.  Maybe I could understand you better...if I could *understand* you better?

**ANGEL.**  Go on man, I'd like to see the girl go all urban. It'd be great for a laugh.

**AMY.** *(Really trying to connect with him.)* Yeah, I can get raise the roof. I can roll with the homies. Was that right? *(Others laugh or get nervous for her etc.)*

**DEREK.** *(Laughing)* Girl, you're still crazy but I'll give you some cool points for tryin.

**AMY.** *(Proudly to group.)* I got some cool points, yo! Foshizzle! What'd I just say?

**DEREK.** I have no idea.

*(All break up into groups to discuss project. AMY goes to JAKE.)*

**AMY.** *(Still trying to be cool with her slang.)* So, Jake…is your knee still harshin' you, man?

**JAKE.** What?

**AMY.** *(Dropping the 'cool' talk.)* How's your knee?

**JAKE.** Do you have any idea how many times a day someone asks me that?

**AMY.** A lot?

**JAKE.** Yeah, a lot!

**AMY.** So, You gonna be back for the state championship?

**JAKE.** No! The knee is totally blown.

**AMY.** Won't it be better by then? They can't win it without you.

**JAKE.** Well guess what! They're gonna have to. My career is over…my life is over.

**JANE.** *(Sweetly, sincerely.)* Hey, let it go. A bum knee's not all that bad…

**JAKE.** You, little Miss Happy Pants, don't get it! My whole life has revolved around sports. Ever since I was little I was on some team or another. The only time my dad showed me any kind of, you know… *(Uncomfortable)*

**TEACHER.** Affection…

**JAKE.** Yeah, was when we won a game. Then he was the proud father.

**TEACHER.** I'm sorry Jake.

**JAKE.** No, at least it was something…but now I've blown out my knee, lost my free ride at State…I have nothing. I am nothing.

**TEACHER.** Surely there's…

**JAKE.** No…you don't get it either. There is only football. I'm not the smart guy, I'm not the rich *(Or "hot".)* guy…I was the guy who threw the touchdown pass that won the game…I was the football hero. Now when people see me they'll say didn't you *used* to be somebody? Pathetic.

**AMY.** Hey, Jake. There's more to life than football.

**JAKE.** Well I sure don't see it.

**TEACHER.** I see a man who has infinite possibilities. A man who has the chance to redefine his course in life.

**JAKE.** I wish I saw what you see.

**JANE.** You can see it if you want to.

**JAKE.** Could you just leave me alone…all of you…please?
*(JAKE is frustrated & afraid there is no future.  He is without direction and feels he will 'disappear' because he's no longer special.)*

### #3 Sound Cue:  *"SO MUCH MORE"*

**JAKE.**
IF I'D HAVE BEEN A LITTLE STRONGER, THEN MAYBE I
    WOULD STILL BE A HERO
I HELD THE BALL A SECOND LONGER THAN I SHOULD,
    TOOK A HIT AND NOW I'M A ZERO
AND I HAD IT ALL PLANNED OUT; I HAD WHAT IT TOOK
    TO BE A WINNER
BUT THEN MY LUCK RAN OUT – NOW I DON'T KNOW
    WHO I AM
SO WHERE'S MY PURPOSE?  THERE'S NO MORE MEANING
IT'S LIKE EVERYTHING I HAVE BUILT MY LIFE ON IS SUD-
    DENLY GONE
I'VE LOST DIRECTION – THERE'S NO CONNECTION
MY DREAM IS DEAD – NOW FATE HAS SLAMMED THE
    DOOR
I COULDA BEEN SO MUCH MORE

JANE. You know, for every door that closes…
JAKE. Yeah, yeah…I've heard that one.

*(Sings)*
ANYBODY WANNA SEE A MAGIC TRICK?
CAUSE HERE'S A MAN WHO'S SLOWLY DISAPPEARING
IF NOT FOR THIS, I WOULDA BEEN A FIRST-ROUND PICK
HEY, DON'T YOU FIND MY SULKING SO ENDEARING?
WE ALL HAVE FACES WE WEAR; WE EACH HAVE A ROLE
    TO PLAY
BUT I EXPECTED LIFE TO BE FAIR…GUESS THAT WAS MY
    MISTAKE

**TEACHER.** You're right, Jake.  We do have roles we play, but
they aren't *all* we are.

**LUKE.** Yeah, bro. We're all good at different stuff. Your talent is just one aspect of you.

**AMY.** *(Kidding around.)* That's true. I'm a very good shopper, for example, but I like to think there's a deeper level!

**DEREK.** *(Messing with AMY.)* Yeah, well *thinkin'* it don't make it so! *(AMY hits him pretending to be mad.)*

**TEACHER.** *(Trying to ignore the antics.)* Seriously, Jake…think about it.

**JAKE.**
CAN I FIND MY PURPOSE — FIND NEW MEANING?

**ANGEL.**
EVERYBODY HAS A DEMON THEY'RE TRYING TO SHAKE

**TEACHER.**
RELEASE YOUR SORROW – THERE'S STILL TOMORROW

**LUKE.**
LET'S FORGET THE LABELS WE HAVE WORN BEFORE

**JANE.**
CAUSE AREN'T WE ALL SO MUCH MORE?

**JAKE.**
I'LL NEVER BE THE MAN I WAS BEFORE…

**TEACHER.**
BUT YOU CAN BE SO MUCH MORE.

*(TEACHER holds football right in JAKE'S face.)*

**TEACHER.** What do you see?

**JAKE.** Well, duh, it's a football.

**TEACHER.** What else do you see?

**JAKE.** Nothing, just a football.

**TEACHER.** Take 5 steps back. *(He does.)* Now what do you see?

**JAKE.** A smaller football…Okay, the room, Skye, Luke, the desks, the trees outside, *(Points to audience member.)* that really cute girl over there.

**TEACHER.** See, when you focus too hard on 1 thing you miss out on everything else.

**JAKE.** What does that mean?

**TEACHER.** *(Takes on a mysterious accent like a Kung Fu master imparting wisdom on his pupil.)* Whatever you want it to mean, Grasshopper.

**AMY.** It means there's more to life than football.

**TEACHER.** Gather around. Let's work on some ideas.

*(TEACHER gathers students at table. AMY notices DEREK sitting, S.R. alone — she goes to sit with him.)*

**AMY.** *(To DEREK.)* You know this is the first time you've spoken to me since 6th grade.

**DEREK.** Well, you got all popular, know what I'm sayin?

**AMY.** And…well, you got all…*(Indicates his gang clothing & rough exterior.)*

**DEREK.** Whatever…I mean, hey you're a cheerleader, V. P. of the class, drama club and all that. *(AMY is in a stunned silence.)* I do read the school paper.

**AMY.** Ha, you're the only one. *(Uncomfortable pause.)* And well, you've got your *(Does quotation marks in air.)* 'posse'.

**DEREK.** Yeah, but…

**AMY.** But what?

**DEREK.** Never mind.

**AMY.** *(Sincerely)* C'mon.

**DEREK.** Okay. It's like this. I mean yeah, I got my crew and they're my boys and all…but…it's like they just wanna roll round the block in their wips flashin their dubs. The block ain't enough for me. The world is bigger than a city block and I wanna get me a piece of it when I graduate. Like George Bernard Shaw said, "If you take too long in deciding what to do with your life, you'll find you've done it."

**AMY.** Wow, that was deep.

**DEREK.** Just don't tell any of my *(Does quotation marks in air.)* "posse".

**AMY.** Those guys are…

**DEREK.** Wack?

**AMY.** Yeah, wack. Why do you hang out with them anyway?

**DEREK.** To survive. It's hard to be in someone's way when you're standin' next to them...

**AMY.** Aren't you scared?

**DEREK.** It don't matter. Once you're in, they don't just let you out. Besides, I figure "What does not destroy me, makes me stronger." Nietzsche.

**JANE.** *(Overhearing their conversation.)* Did he just quote Shaw & Nietzsche?

**TEACHER.** I believe he did.

**LUKE.** Derek, it may be a risk to leave this gang...but it's a bigger risk to stay in.

**DEREK.** I can't just walk...I *don't* have a choice.

**LUKE.** Wrong. "What it lies in our power to do, it lies in our power *not* to do." That's Aristotle.

**ALL.** *(Impressed)* Aristotle.

**DEREK.** *(Agreeing)* I hear ya. *(Challenging LUKE with quotes.)* Okay, get this. It's like Erica Jong said, "If you don't risk anything you risk even more."

**ALL.** *(Ad libs — impressed.)* All right Derek.

**LUKE.** Okay, I've got one. The reality is "...doing what's right is no guarantee against misfortune." That's William McFee.

**SKYE.** William McFee. Who's William McFee?

**JAKE.** *(JAKE steps between DEREK and LUKE and announces.)* "A spoon full of sugar helps the medicine go down." Mary Poppins. *(All groan, laugh, shoo him away — JAKE is proud.)* Thank you! Thank you very much! Pretty funny, huh?

**LUKE.** *(Sincerely)* "The time is always right to do what is right." Martin Luther King, Jr.

**TEACHER.** *(Approving)* Alright!

**DEREK.** I wish it was that easy.

**LUKE.** *(Understanding DEREK'S situation.)* Yeah.

**AMY.** *(Aside, to DEREK.)* That was impressive. Where'd you get all that?

**DEREK.** I read. Ayight? Now, c'mon girl, it's your turn. You gotta have some secrets?

**AMY.** *(Pauses — it looks like she's gonna open up.)* Promise you won't tell?

**DEREK.** I never told anyone you had that crush on coach Douglas.

**JANE.** *(Overhearing)* I had a crush on Coach Douglas.

**SKYE.** Me too

**ANGEL.** Me too

**JAKE.** All the girls did

**AMY.** *(Embarrassed)* Ooooh, I hate you for remembering that …Okay…here it is…you know those strips people put on their nose to get rid of zits?

**DEREK.** Yeah, they look like Band-Aids.

**AMY.** Well, I'm obsessed with them because I have this fear of getting a giant nose zit.

**DEREK.** *(Laughing)* Oh, man, that ain't right.

**AMY.** Remember, don't tell. *(Leaves DEREK to join the rest of the group.)*

**DEREK.** *(To himself.)* Who you gonna tell that to?

**AMY.** Come on. Let's get to work.

**JANE.** *(Taking charge — energized.)* Okay, guys, we've gotta focus on the project…it's due on Monday. So, what do we do for our presentation? It's gotta be big!

**SKYE.** *(Overly dramatic.)* I picture a multimedia blitz, video, songs, dancing, PowerPoint presentation, interactive comedy…

**ANGEL.** Uh, hello! It's due Monday.

**SKYE.** Okay, well, a skit, drawings…sock puppets?.

**ANGEL.** *(Trying to get thru to her.)* Monday.

**DEREK.** What about a song? That sounds tight — we could do that.

**LUKE.** Yeah, right. Who's gonna listen to a bunch of high-schoolers singing a song? *(All do a slow look toward audience then snap back.)* Let's think.

**AMY.** Come on girls, let's think. We need an idea.

**JAKE.** What about the guys?

**AMY.** Pffft. We'll do this. All you guys think about is sports anyway.

**GUYS.** *(Wounded)* Ow.

**SKYE.** No, they think about so much more than sports…there's se…

*(Starts to say 'sex' but never quite gets it out.)*

**JAKE.** Don't say it.

**SKYE.** Sports….and se….

**JAKE.** Zippit.

**SKYE.** Food…sports and of course se…

**JAKE.** Zip…zippola…zipperini…Okay, what about girls? What do they think about? Cuz I have no idea.

**DEREK.** I'm stayin out of this one.

**LUKE.** Guys…shoes…diets…shopping…fuzzy little kittens and guys.

**DEREK.** Look Dog, you gotta admit they are a little more well rounded than we are.

**LUKE.** Derek…you're not helping.

**JANE.** Ms Watson, can you break down the fundamental difference between guys & girls.

**TEACHER.** *(With confidence, as if there is a good answer.)* …No. *(She goes back to her desk.)*

**DEREK.** Ayight ladies, I'll admit that guys aren't too bright.

**LUKE & JAKE.** Hey, wait a min…

**DEREK.** Present company excluded…but ladies, help us out…don't play any mind games with us. We ain't got the gear.

**GIRLS.** Mind games? Like what?

**DEREK.** Okay, I've got a mind game for you. *(Whispers plan to JAKE. DEREK & JAKE take on role of a couple & act this one out. JAKE grabs a chair & sits center. DEREK uses his best high, 'female' voice & sassy walk.)* Pooh bear, do I need to lose weight?

**JAKE.** *(As the man in front of TV with remote control.)* No, baby, you're beautiful just the way you are.

**DEREK.** *(As the woman.)* Xskew me, Xskew me. Just the way I am? What is that supposed to mean?

**JAKE.** Nothin', nothin' you're beautiful. Don't change a thing.

**DEREK.** Maybe just lose 2 pounds?

**JAKE.** No babe, you're perfect.

**DEREK.** Just 2 ittle, wittle pounds?

**JAKE.** Okay, maybe just 2 pounds.

**DEREK.** YOU THINK I'M FAT!! *(Drops character & turns back to girls.)* That is just wrong. *(DEREK & JAKE are proud of themselves — triumphant — they enjoyed teasing the girls.)*

**AMY.** Okay, I've got one. What about this for a mind game?

**GIRLS.** *(Ad libs.)* You show 'em, Amy. Go Amy.

**AMY.** *(AMY acts out a guy & girl on a date, changing her voice for each.)* *(Girl)* No, that's enough. *(Guy)* Oh, c'mon baby, do it for me. *(Girl)* No, I'm not ready. *(Guy)* But baby, I love you…I'll love you forever. *(Girl)* I said no. *(Guy)* If you love me, you'll do it…Then the next day he's gone and the girls pregnant. *(Drops character & turns back to group.)* Now THAT is wrong.

*(ALL. Silent, stunned, uncomfortable.)*

**JAKE.** So, what do girls want?

### #4 Sound Cue: *"COMMUNICATION BREAKDOWN"*

*(Comic song about boy/girl relationships. It becomes a competition of point-of-view. A playful, challenge with girls pitted against guys — also has truth in it.)*

**JANE.** Girls want someone to share their thoughts and feelings with.
**SKYE.** Someone to hold their hand.
**AMY.** A shoulder to rest her head on!
**ANGEL.** An emotional equal to share life experiences.
**AMY.** But let's face it — the emotional equal of a teenage boy is a tadpole!
**LUKE.** *(Over the top.)* Yeah, but tadpoles are sooo cute!!
**AMY.** Maybe in a pond, but who wants to date one?
**SKYE.** Eeew!  Tadpoles look like little sp…*(Was going to say "sperm".)*
**ALL.** *(Cutting her off.)* No.
**AMY.** *(Spoken)* You know that boys *cannot* communicate!

**JAKE.**
*(Sung)* BUT GIRLS THINK THEY KNOW EVERYTHING!

**SKYE.** *(Spoken)* We do!

**JANE.**
*(Sung))* ALL THE PROBLEMS GUYS CREATE!

**DEREK.** *(Spoken)* Hey, don't look at us...the problem starts with you!

**BOYS.**
*(Sung)* GIRLS LIVE ON VENUS

**GIRLS.**
*(Sung)* BOYS COME FROM MARS

**BOYS.**
*(Sung)* GIRLS LIKE THEIR LIPSTICK

**GIRLS.**
*(Sung)*AND BOYS LIKE FAST CARS.  BOYS HIDE THEIR
     FEELINGS...

**BOYS.**
*(Sung)* GIRLS SHOW THEM ALL!

**GIRLS.** *(Spoken, imitating BOYS.)* We just wanna watch the game!
**BOYS.** *(Mocking GIRLS with high voice.)* We just need a mall!

**GIRLS.**
*(Sung)* ALL GUYS HAVE A ONE-TRACK MIND; THEY
WANNA SEE HOW FAR WE'LL GO

**BOYS.**
*(Sung)* AND ALL GIRLS CAN SAY IS "NO, NO – NO, NO, NO"

**ALL.**
*(Sung)* GUESS IT'S A LOST CAUSE; EACH DAY WE LOSE
     GROUND
THE OPPOSITE SEX IS A MYSTERY – COMMUNICATION
     BREAKDOWN!

**BOYS.**
*(Chant/Sung)* I HEAR YOU TALKIN' BUT IT MIGHT AS
WELL BE PORTUGUESE BUT THEN YOU LOOK SO FINE,

BRINGS ME DOWN TO MY KNEES

**GIRLS.**
*(Chant/Sung)* MAYBE YOU WOULD UNDERSTAND IF
YOU WOULD EVER LISTEN AND…
SHOW A LITTLE AFFECTION, BUT YOU CAN'T CAUSE
    YOU'RE A MAN

**DEREK.**
*(Rap)* CAN'T LIVE WITH OR WITHOUT, SO WE POUT – WE
ARGUE AND SHOUT AND WE DOUBT
IT'S A DISASTER, BUT YOU ASK HER TO TAKE YOU BACK
AND THE FASTER YOU TRY TO MAKE UP, YOU BREAK UP
    – SO WAKE UP, IT'S A GAME
LIKE OIL AND WATER, WE DON'T MIX…AND IT'S ALWAYS
    THE SAME

**BOYS.**
*(Sung)* GIRLS LIVE ON VENUS

**GIRLS.**
*(Sung)* BOYS COME FROM MARS

**BOYS.**
*(Sung)* GIRLS CRAVE MILK CHOCOLATE

**GIRLS.**
*(Sung)* AND BOYS DIG LOUD GUITARS.  BOYS HIDE THEIR
    FEELINGS…

**BOYS.**
*(Sung)* GIRLS SHOW THEM ALL!

    **GIRLS.** *(Spoken, imitating BOYS.)* We don't admit our weak-
nesses.
    **BOYS.** *(Mocking GIRLS with high voice.)* We can't even throw
a ball!

**GIRLS.**
*(Sung)* ALL GUYS HAVE A ONE-TRACK MIND; THEY
WANNA SEE HOW FAR WE'LL GO

**BOYS.**
*(Sung)* AND ALL GIRLS CAN SAY IS "NO, NO – NO, NO, NO"

**ALL.**
*(Sung)* GUESS IT'S A LOST CAUSE; EACH DAY WE LOSE
   GROUND
THE OPPOSITE SEX IS A MYSTERY – COMMUNICATION
   BREAKDOWN!
COMMUNICATION BREAK…*(CAST freezes in mid-word.)*

**AMY.** *(Spoken with underscore — AMY steps out of song. DEREK notices her standing alone & he slowly walks toward her, listening. AMY doesn't see him. She is talking to herself.)* They're all laughing and cutting up, but it's all too real to me. I'm the one that didn't say 'no' quite enough. I thought that just once would be OK. But it's not. Once is all it takes. How'd I let him change my mind? *(Pause)* Wow. Things like this happen to other people, not to me. I'm way too young. I have way too many plans for my life. I can't have a baby now. What am I gonna do?...Quit school & raise a baby alone? Ask my parents to raise it?...Put it up for adoption?...Have an abor…? There's no easy choice. I'm smart. Why didn't I think about that before? How am I gonna tell my parents? What will everybody say? Just like that, I'm pregnant. And what if I got some disease? Oh, man.

**DEREK.** *(Spoken)* Who you gonna tell that to?

**AMY.** *(Startled, realizing DEREK just heard all that.)* I guess I just told you.

**DEREK.** What now?

**AMY.** I don't know. *(Full of regret, angry with herself.)* It's my life…I should have been in control. Why didn't I just say no? No. I'm not going to mess up my life. No. I'm not giving in to that game. No. I'm not compromising myself. No! Why didn't I do that? *(She sobs in DEREK'S arms.)*

*(DEREK comforts AMY. They do not rejoin the group. Cast unfreezes as the fast music warps back in. AMY slowly collects herself. Her mood is much more somber in comparison to the rest of the group.)*

**GIRLS.**
*(Sung)* ALL GUYS HAVE A ONE-TRACK MIND; THEY WANNA SEE HOW FAR WE'LL GO

**BOYS.**
*(Sung)* AND ALL GIRLS CAN SAY IS "NO, NO – NO, NO, NO"

**ALL.**
*(Sung)* GUESS IT'S A LOST CAUSE; EACH DAY WE LOSE
    GROUND
THE OPPOSITE SEX IS A MYSTERY – COMMUNICATION
    BREAKDOWN!

*(Cast laughs and carries on as music goes out. AMY still looks to be somewhere else.)*

**TEACHER.** *(Quietly, to AMY.)* Are you okay?
**AMY.** *(Somber)* Yeah, I'm fine.
**TEACHER.** *(Loudly, to group.)* Okay, game over. Truce in the battle of the sexes. Game over.
**JAKE.** It may be over but we still won.
**ANGEL.** C'mon Ms Watson, you're old…*(Group gasps. TEACHER gives playful glare.)* Uh…Old-ER…*(Another glare.)* than we are. What's the deal with boys and girls?
**TEACHER.** *(STUDENTS freeze. Speaking to audience.)* I am not equipped to deal with this one. The only Long-term relationship I've had was…*(Realizing)* I haven't had a long-term relationship. All right…men & women…here goes. *(Break freeze. Addresses STUDENTS.)* Okay, *(Pause)* men AND women are a mystery… *(To audience.)* I am so totally making this up. *(To students)* Men & women are a mystery, but one day you'll find someone who understands your mystery and you'll get theirs. *(All have blank stares)*
**JAKE.** A mystery? Like Scooby Doo? *(All groan.)*
**TEACHER.** *(Playfully)* Maybe in your world and that's fine. *(Changing the subject.)* Now, back to the project. What have you got so far?

**SKYE.** *(Trying to keep the mood playful with a touch of sarcasm.)* Okay, let's see…*(To AMY.)* She's rollin' with the homies, Jakes got football head, *(To ANGEL.)* her parents are bums and guys are scum…that's it in a nutshell.

**JANE.** *(Suddenly gets idea — jumps up.)* Wait! Jake didn't always have football head.

**ALL.** What?

**JANE.** Stay right here. I'll be right back… *(EXITS)*

**ALL.** *(Ad-libs)* What's she doing? Who knows? Where'd she go? Etc.

**DEREK.** Hey, she gets to leave…can I leave?

**TEACHER.** No.

**JANE.** *(Still talking off stage.)* Just running to my locker. Don't start without me…almost got it. I'm coming. Hang on. Be right there…Okay, I'm back. *(Holds up journal.)* I've got *'the list'*.

**AMY.** *(They all realize what she has.)* No! Gimme that. No one needs to read that.

**ANGEL.** Cool, let me see it.

**JAKE.** Yeah, give it up.

**DEREK.** Please bury the thing.

*(All ad-libs & commotion trying to get the journal out of JANE'S hand. JANE runs behind TEACHER's desk and climbs up on chair and then on top of desk.)*

**JANE.** I didn't want to do this, but…

**TEACHER.** Okay, I'll admit I'm clueless.

**JANE.** *(Explaining to TEACHER.)* Okay, the summer after 2nd grade we all made a list of what we wanted to be when we grow up AND we promised to be friends forever. Now let's read this and see what we said. I'll read Jake's first. Jake wanted to be…

**ALL.** *(Ad-libs, guessing.)* Football hero, sports star, coach, jock.

**JANE.** Nope…he wanted to be a drummer in a Rock & Roll band.

**ALL.** *(Ad-libs)* What? No way? Really? Cool!

**JAKE.** I'd forgotten all about that. Sweet.

**JANE.** Okay, Angel, you wanted to be a preschool teacher.

**ANGEL.** *(Quietly)* Yeah.

ALL. Whoa.

JANE. Amy, you wanted to be…

AMY. No, don't say it!!  Don't say it!

JANE.  Barbie!

ALL. *(Laughing)* Barbie?!

AMY.  *(Embarrassed)* Can I change that?

ALL. Please do.

JANE. Derek wanted to be a ballerina.

DEREK. *(Freaks out — leaps over desks to get that book.)* I never said 'ballerina'.

SKYE. *(Grabs book & reads.)* No, but you did say "Ballet Guy".

DEREK. Hey, dancers are very athletic…and they get to pick up pretty girls all day.

JAKE. *(Likes the 'picking up pretty girls' idea.)* Ballet guy…I never thought about it like that. Cool.

SKYE. Jane wanted to be a counselor for troubled youth.

ANGEL. She's always been that…Miss Mary Sunshine…spreading mirth & joy.

JANE. *(Takes book back, continues reading.)* Luke wanted to do puppet shows for children in 3rd world countries.

ALL.  What? Puppet shows?

SKYE. *(Teasing)* Sock puppets?

LUKE. Look, I wanted to help people. I still do. Maybe not with sock puppets. But I'd like to make a difference. I believe we're all on the planet to help each other out…in fact I'd like to join the Peace Corps or something after graduation…but man, my family has other ideas.

DEREK. Yo, your old man helps people.  Ain't he some hotshot spleen surgeon or something like that?

LUKE.  Yeah.

ANGEL. Well…then he helps people right?

LUKE.  Yeah, if they pay their bills…but when it comes to my dreams…he…

DEREK. He what?

LUKE. Nah, it's…

DEREK. Say it.  What about your dreams?

LUKE.  He thinks I'm wasting my life. To him, rewards are something you count in the bank…to me, helping people IS the reward.

**DEREK.**  What do you have to say about that?

**LUKE.**  Well...

**DEREK.** *(Pushes LUKE.)* C'mon.  How's that make you feel when your parents dis your dreams?

### #5 Sound Cue: *"BLEEDING HEART"*

**LUKE.** I'm just frustrated, alright? They mean well, but...I don't know...

*(LUKE is a centered, good guy.  People expect him to act a certain way.  He is having trouble breaking out of his expected role and revealing his frustrations.)*

**LUKE.**
SO SICK AND TIRED...OF PLAYIN OUT SOMEBODY ELSE'S
FANTASY

**DEREK.**
UH, YEAH, I GOTTA GET FREE

**LUKE.**
I'M ABOUT THE GIVING, BUT IT SEEMS THAT THEY'VE
MADE OTHER PLANS FOR ME

**DEREK.**
THEY DON'T UNDERSTAND MY DESTINY

**LUKE.**
MONEY DOESN'T DRIVE ME; THEY CAN HAVE THEIR
    EMPTY LIFE,
THEIR LACK OF TRUST AND TOLERANCE, IT CUTS ME
    LIKE A KNIFE

**DEREK.**
YEAH IT CUTS ME LIKE A KNIFE

**LUKE.**
MY BLEEDING HEART IS LIKE AN OCEAN, DEEP WITH

PASSION AND DEVOTION
LOOK AT ALL THIS SUFFERING – I'M BOUND TO DO MY
    PART
AND I CURSE THE BOX THEY HOLD ME IN; THEY NEVER
    LISTEN, NEVER BEND
BUT I WILL WIN CAUSE CHANGE BEGINS IN EVERY
    BLEEDING HEART

DRUG-ADDICTED BABIES, AIRPLANES CRASHED WITH
    VENGEANCE THROUGH OUR DREAMS OF PEACE
DISMISS AND MOCK MY INNOCENCE, BUT I BELIEVE
    WITH LOVE ALL HATE CAN CEASE

**DEREK.**
SO I KEEP THE FAITH AND CONTROL THE GRIEF

**LUKE.**
MY PARENTS WON'T SUPPORT THE THINGS THEY FAIL TO
UNDERSTAND

**DEREK.**
WHY CAN'T THEY UNDERSTAND?

**LUKE.**
YES, IT'S SAFER ON THE SIDELINES, BUT THAT'S NOT
WHO I AM

**DEREK.**
WISH I COULD TAKE MY LIFE INTO MY OWN HANDS

**LUKE.**
MY BLEEDING HEART IS LIKE AN OCEAN, DEEP WITH
    PASSION AND DEVOTION
LOOK AT ALL THIS SUFFERING (DEREK. ALL AROUND
    THE WORLD) – I'M BOUND TO DO MY PART
(DEREK. WHEN DOES IT END?) AND I CURSE THE BOX
    THEY HOLD ME IN (DEREK. NO WAY OUT)
THEY NEVER LISTEN, NEVER BEND (DEREK. THEY FILL
    ME UP WITH DOUBT)

BUT I WILL WIN CAUSE CHANGE BEGINS IN EVERY
    BLEEDING HEART

MY FOLKS MEAN WELL; I LOVE AND FORGIVE THEM
BUT DAMN, I'VE SEEN ENOUGH STARVING CHILDREN
I DON'T WANT A MANSION UP ON THE HILL

> **ALL.**
> *(Sung)* I JUST WANNA KEEP IT REAL

> **LUKE.**
> *(Sung)* STOP WAVING BENJAMINS IN MY FACE

> **ALL.**
> I'M A PROUD CITIZEN OF THE HUMAN RACE
> SO BEFORE YOU IGNORE ME, LET ME GET THIS OUT:

> **LUKE.**
> *(Spoken)* YOU ONLY GET ONE LIFE, SO I'M MAKING MINE
> COUNT
> *(Sung)* SO LABEL ME A "BLEEDING HEART" – I'VE BEEN
>     CALLED THAT NAME BEFORE

> **DEREK.**
> CAN'T LET IT GET ME DOWN

> **LUKE.**
> BUT I'M CONVINCED THIS WORLD WE SHARE COULD
>     USE A COUPLE MORE

> **DEREK.**
> AND WE COULD PRACTICE LOVE, NOT WAR

> **LUKE.**
> MY BLEEDING HEART IS LIKE AN OCEAN, DEEP WITH
>     PASSION AND DEVOTION
> LOOK AT ALL THIS SUFFERING (DEREK. ALL AROUND
> THE WORLD) – I'M BOUND TO DO MY PART
> (DEREK. WHEN DOES IT END?) AND I CURSE THE BOX

THEY HOLD ME IN (DEREK. NO WAY OUT)
THEY NEVER LISTEN, NEVER BEND (DEREK. THEY FILL
    ME UP WITH DOUBT)
BUT I WILL WIN CAUSE CHANGE BEGINS IN EVERY
    BLEEDING HEART

**JANE.** Hey Luke, your parents will come around.

**ANGEL.** At least they care enough to want what's best for you.

**LUKE.** Yeah, they'll get it someday.

**ANGEL.** Sure they will.

**LUKE.** *(Lightening up-smiles.)* Course I'll be 30 by then…but hey, it'll happen.

**JAKE.** *(Matter-of-fact)* What about Skye? What did you wanna be?

**SKYE.** *(Adamant)* It doesn't matter.

**JAKE.** Sure it does.

**SKYE.** *(Quietly, intensely pleads with JANE for support.)* Jane, please.

**JANE.** *(Realizing SKYE is serious.)* If Skye says 'no'…that's her choice.

**AMY.** Sure…SHE gets to say no.

**SKYE.** *(Angry)* What does that mean?

**AMY.** *(Covering)* It uh, means that everybody is opening up…and you should too.

**SKYE.** *(Defeated)* Go on, read it.

**ANGEL.** What did she want to be?

**JANE.** *(Stunned pause-reading SKYE'S words.)* She wanted to be "somebody else…anybody else."

**JAKE.** *(Gentle & sincere.)* You wanted to be 'somebody else'? Why? You're funny & pretty…*(He approaches & gently brushes hair out of her eyes and goes to embrace her. She rejects his affection — she's uncomfortable & shrugs to get his hands off of her.)* What is it Skye? *(JAKE is still trying to gently embrace her.)*

**SKYE.** *(Over-reacting.)* Stop!

**JAKE.** *(Not understanding.)* What? What'd I do?

**SKYE.** Just stop! Leave me alone! *(JAKE gently touches her shoulder to turn her around — he's confused. She explodes…and over reacts, batting his arms away from her.)* Don't touch me, get away! Get away! I said, leave me alone!

### #6 Sound Cue: *"STOP (PART ONE)"*

**TEACHER.** *(ENTERS urgently — trying to assess the situation. Speaks over music.)* Skye, what's going on?

**SKYE.** *(Distraught)* I don't want him to touch me. He shouldn't be doing that. He won't stop! Even if I fight, he won't stop.

**JAKE.** What did I do?

**TEACHER.** Who, Skye? Jake?

**SKYE.** No, not Jake...my step-father! *(Everyone is stunned. SKYE is falling apart.)* My step-father won't stop! I can hear him coming down the hall and I pretend to be asleep, but he keeps coming. He comes in and sits on the bed and I can smell the liquor on his breath. He calls me his "little lady" and then...then...It's so wrong. *(She breaks down.)* Oh God, I think I'm gonna be sick.

**TEACHER.** Nobody should have to deal with that.
*(Sung)*
HOW HAVE YOU KEPT THIS INSIDE FOR SO LONG?

**SKYE.** *(Spoken)* Cause I feel lost and ashamed.

**AMY.** *(Spoken)* Why? You did nothing wrong!

**TEACHER.** *(Spoken gently)* This has to stop.

**ENSEMBLE**
*(Sung)* STOP THE BLEEDING — STOP THE VIOLENCE
STOP THE INSANITY – BREAK THE SILENCE
NOBODY HAS THE RIGHT TO BREAK YOU DOWN
STOP THE FEAR; DON'T RUN OR COWER
THE TIME IS NOW TO TAKE BACK THE POWER
TAKE THIS LIFELINE – WE WON'T LET YOU DROWN

**GIRLS.**
BUT HE'LL GO ON AND ON AND ON AND ON AND ON...

**GUYS.**
HE'LL GO ON AND ON AND ON AND ON AND ON

**GIRLS.**
HE'LL GO ON AND ON AND ON...

**ALL.**
UNTIL YOU MAKE HIM STOP!

**LUKE.**
*(Sung)* IT'S TIME TO SET THIS RIGHT.

**SKYE.** *(Spoken)* No, you guys don't understand.

**JAKE & JANE.**
*(Sung)* WE'RE GONNA BE RIGHT THERE TO HELP YOU
THROUGH!

**SKYE.** *(Spoken)* I can't, I won't!  I'd rather die!
**ANGEL.** *(Spoken)* You're *already* dying inside.

**TEACHER.**
*(Sung)* IT'S GONNA BE ALRIGHT – THERE ARE THINGS
THAT WE CAN DO.

**LUKE.** *(Aside, to the other guys.)* Man I thought my problems
were bad.
    **JAKE.** Yeah, I feel like such a fool.
    **DEREK.** Yo, this dude needs to pay…period!  This just ain't
cool.
    **TEACHER.** You *can* stop this.

*(Dance Break.)*

**ENSEMBLE.**
*(Sung)*
STOP THE BLEEDING — STOP THE VIOLENCE
(**SKYE.** HOW?)
STOP THE INSANITY — BREAK THE SILENCE
(**SKYE.** I CAN'T!)
NOBODY HAS THE RIGHT TO BREAK YOU DOWN
(**SKYE.**  I W, BUT I'M SO AFRAID!)
STOP THE FEAR; DON'T RUN OR COWER
THE TIME IS NOW TO TAKE BACK THE POWER
TAKE THIS  LIFELINE – WE  WON'T  LET  YOU  DROWN

(SKYE. PROMISE ME!)

**GIRLS.**
BUT HE'LL GO ON AND ON AND ON AND ON AND ON…

**GUYS.**
HE'LL GO ON AND ON AND ON AND ON AND ON

**GIRLS.**
HE'LL GO ON AND ON AND ON…

**ALL.**
UNTIL YOU MAKE HIM STOP…STOP!

**TEACHER.** That's it Skye!  It ends right here.  It ends NOW! You have to tell your mother.
**SKYE.** I told her…she didn't believe ME, she believed HIM. She chose that sicko over her own daughter.  I'm so humiliated, I'm so ashamed. *(Sobs)*
**TEACHER.** You didn't ask for this — this is not your fault — there is no reason to be ashamed.
**JAKE.** Why don't you get out of there?
**AMY.** You can stay at my house.
**TEACHER.**  Skye, you got a bum deal and this isn't going to be easy.  In fact — this is gonna be the hardest thing you'll ever have to face…but it has to be done and you'll make it. There are places to go. There are crisis centers-but first we're going to the police.  This man needs to be in jail. I'll go with you.
**SKYE.** You don't understand…if I leave, he said he'd go after my little sister. She's only seven.  The same age I was when…*(She can't finish the sentence.)*

**#7 Sound Cue: *"STOP! (PART TWO-REPRISE)"***

*(Dialogue with musical underscoring.)*

**TEACHER.** Oh, my God.
**SKYE.** I just can't do it.
**(FEMALE) TEACHER.** Skye, you have to tell — if not to

protect yourself, then to protect your little sister!  What's to stop him from going after her even if you *are* there?  This is bigger than just you.  Come here…let me tell you about my greatest regret in life.  When I was a little girl, my best friend and I sneaked out of her house at midnight and walked across the street to the school playground.  We just wanted to hang out on the swings.  This eighteen-year-old guy came up and grabbed me — my friend thought he was joking around — she thought it was funny and she ran home without me.  Then the guy banged my head on the stairs, ripped my clothes and started to rape me.  I was able to get free and kick him where it hurts!  And I got away.

***Alternate Dialogue:***

**(MALE) TEACHER.**  Skye, you have to tell — if not to protect yourself, then to protect your little sister!  What's to stop him from going after her even if you *are* there?  This is bigger than just you.  Come here…let me tell you about my greatest regret in life.  When my little sister was 12, she & her best friend sneaked out of the house at midnight and walked across the street to the school playground. They just wanted to hang out on the swings. This eighteen-year-old guy came up and grabbed my sister — her friend thought he was joking around – she thought it was funny and ran home & left my sister. The guy banged her head on the stairs, ripped her clothes and started to rape her.  She was able to get free and kick him where it hurts!  She got away.

    **LUKE.** Way to go, Ms. Watson!

    **ANGEL.** Dead on!

    **JAKE.** Alright!

    **TEACHER.** But wait a minute…

*(Sung)*

I MADE ONE HUGE MISTAKE…I NEVER TOLD A SOUL
AND I KNEW THIS GUY'S NAME AND I KNEW WHERE HE
    LIVED!
HE DID THIS AWFUL CRIME, AND I LET HIM WALK AWAY
I SHOULD HAVE TOLD, BUT NOW IT'S MUCH TOO LATE

*(Dialogue)*

**ANGEL.** So why didn't you?

**(FEMALE) TEACHER.** I sneaked out of my house that day and was afraid of getting in trouble. I told no one — not even my friend that ran away. And here's the real tragedy. Two weeks later, the same guy brutally raped another girl. I might have prevented that, had I told. That's why this man must be stopped, Skye! It's up to you. Only you can...

*Alternate Dialogue:*

**(MALE) TEACHER.** My sister sneaked out of the house that day and was afraid of getting in trouble. She made me promise not to tell. I told no one. And here's the real tragedy. Two weeks later, the same guy brutally raped another girl. I might have prevented that, had I told. That's why this man must be stopped, Skye! It's up to you. Only you can...

**ENSEMBLE.**
STOP THE BLEEDING — STOP THE VIOLENCE
STOP THE INSANITY – BREAK THE SILENCE
NOBODY HAS THE RIGHT TO BREAK YOU DOWN
STOP THE FEAR; DON'T RUN OR COWER
THE TIME IS NOW TO TAKE BACK THE POWER
TAKE THIS LIFELINE — WE WON'T LET YOU DROWN
BUT HE'LL GO ON AND ON AND ON AND ON AND ON...
(HE'LL GO ON AND ON AND ON AND ON AND ON)
HE'LL GO ON AND ON AND ON...UNTIL YOU MAKE HIM STOP!

*(Dialogue over music tag.)*

**SKYE.** I can't do it alone.
**JANE.** You won't be alone...
**ANGEL.** We're here for you, Skye!
**LUKE.** Yeah, you've got us!
**TEACHER.** *(Gently repeating for emphasis.)* You've got us.

*(Music Out.)*

**SKYE.** I can't ask for help. I don't want everybody in my business.

**TEACHER.** Everybody needs help sometimes…there's no shame in that. Just surround yourself with people who understand. Look, we can't choose our family. Most of us are lucky. We have good families that mean well, even if we don't always see eye to eye *(Glances at LUKE.)*…but, Skye, you weren't so lucky. Everyone in our lives is either trying to pull us up or pull us down. You gotta surround yourself with those that are pulling you up. The most important choice you will ever make is the people you surround yourself with. *(To DEREK.)* You too Derek. *(DEREK walks SR and sits alone.)* The ones that are going to pull you up may be harder to find, but they're worth the search.

**LUKE.** Skye, we'll be here to pull you up girl.

**AMY.** We're here.

**ANGEL.** We got your back, Skye.

**SKYE.** *(Crying, embracing others)* Thanks.

**TEACHER.** *(Notices DEREK sitting alone.)* Hey, Derek, <u>you</u> might rethink the people *you* hang out with.

**JAKE.** Yeah, what are you hanging around with that gang for?

*(All giving DEREK a hard time. Dialogue overlapping.)*

**ANGEL.** What's with that?

**LUKE.** You're too good for that. You're goin' nowhere, man.

**AMY.** You're wastin' your life.

**JAKE.** Derek, you gotta get out. Just walk away.

**JANE.** What a waste! What are you thinking?

**SKYE.** Wake up, Derek.

**DEREK.** *(To group.)* You know what? I didn't come here for this. I'm out. This is just messed up. *(Starts to EXIT.)*

**TEACHER.** Derek, c'mon, look what you guys have done in no time at all…you've found common ground.

**DEREK.** Common ground…that's it? Aw, please, it ain't that simple.

**TEACHER.** Nobody said it was simple — but it should be.

**DEREK.** Well maybe Beyonce should be my girlfriend but she's not. Okay, cool. We all have something in common…but the problem is people don't wanna see that. Yeah, we've all gotta eat, gotta breathe. We've all got dreams...

    **TEACHER.** That's right and if we can...

    **DEREK.** IF we can? OPEN YOUR EYES!! We can't. People don't want common ground. They don't want to be like the guy standing next to them. They want to think they are better than someone or something so they can pump themselves up. Most people don't want someone else standing next to them, because then you have to look them in the eye...Wack!! Man it is just wack. It's bull!

    **TEACHER.** Listen Derek, you just gotta...

    **DEREK.** *(Hand up-makes brake squeal sound.)* Teach, that's you just backin' off.

*(TEACHER indicates to group to leave them alone for a minute. All EXIT except DEREK & TEACHER who move to opposite sides of the room, deep in thought.)*

### #8 Sound Cue: *"WHAT I SEE"*

*(TEACHER frustrated because she hasn't been able to reach this kid. TEACHER does understand him...she was very much like him as a kid and is desperate to get thru to him.)*

**DEREK.**
*(Rap)*
I HEAR HER SPEAKING AND IT'S GOT ME THINKING
BUT TO CHANGE MY WHOLE LIFESTYLE, SHE'S GOTTA
    BE DRINKING
THINKING I'M A LEAVE THE GANG, SHE BETTER THINK
    AGAIN
I GOTTA HUSTLE ON THE STREETS, SO I CAN BE THE
    MAN
IF SHE COULD ONLY SEE, WHERE I'M FROM THERE'S NO
    HOPE
IT'S EITHER DEATH, JAIL, OR JUST SMOKE DOPE
THIS IS NO JOKE, I'M LIVING LIFE SO BROKE
SOMETIMES THIS MADNESS MAKES ME WANNA GO
    POSTAL
SO WHY TRY, TO FIGHT I
DON'T REALLY CARE IF I'M JUST PASSING MY LIFE BY

BUT SHE'S DETERMINED TO MAKE ME THINK I HAVE A
     CHANCE
TO PUT THIS PAIN BEHIND ME WITHOUT A GLANCE
NOW I'M SO CONFUSED, DON'T KNOW WHAT TO DO
SHOULD I STAY IN THE STREETS, OR DO I GO TO SCHOOL?
MY TEACHER WANTS ME TO SUCCEED AND THAT'S SO
     COOL
BUT CAN SHE REALLY SEE THE THINGS THAT I GO
     THROUGH?


**TEACHER.**
*(Sung)*
IF HE COULD ONLY SEE WHAT I SEE, MAYBE HE WOULD
     LISTEN TO ME
I'VE WALKED THE PATH HE'S ON BEFORE; HE IS MEANT
     FOR SO MUCH MORE!
HOW CAN I REACH HIM WHILE THERE'S STILL TIME?
I DON'T WANT HIM LEFT BEHIND
AND HE COULD SET HIS SPIRIT FREE... IF HE COULD
ONLY SEE WHAT I SEE


**TEACHER.** *(Spoken)* Who am I kidding? I can't change this.
I can't even get these kids to see that they're worth anything.
They're not gonna listen to me! *(Frustrated, exasperated, then
addressing herself sarcasticly.)* So why did you bother to become a
teacher? That's a good question Ms Watson! Answer that! Go on
answer. *(Long pause — thoughtful.)* I wanted to make a difference...to open their eyes to see the endless possibilities of a world
that is right there...RIGHT THERE...waiting for them! *(Long
pause.)* You know what? I don't care. Caring is not in my job
description is it? It's my job to pump their heads with knowledge
that will spill right back out after their next test. That's my
job...nothing more. *(Pause)* So why do you teach? Why do you
care?...Because they matter.


**DEREK.**
*(Rap)*
DISCONTENT WITH LIFE, I FIGHT, AND IT BITES, BUT I
     GOTTA DO IT

I'M BETTER THAN THIS, I WISH I'D GET THE CHANCE TO
    PROVE IT
CAN I WIN, LIKE A GRAND CHAMPION?
SHE HAS ME THINKING IF I TRY, THEN IT CAN BE DONE
BUT TELL ME ONE THING, WHAT IF I SIMPLY FAIL…
AND END UP BACK IN THE HOOD, OR THEY BRING ME TO
    JAIL?
WOULD SHE STILL HELP, WHAT CHOICE DO I HAVE?
DOES IT EVEN MATTER?

**TEACHER.** *(Spoken)* The world is yours to grab!

*(Sung)*
IF HE COULD ONLY SEE WHAT I SEE,
MAYBE HE WOULD LISTEN TO ME
I'VE WALKED THE PATH HE'S ON BEFORE;
HE IS MEANT FOR SO MUCH MORE!
HOW CAN I REACH HIM WHILE THERE'S STILL TIME?
I DON'T WANT HIM LEFT BEHIND
AND HE COULD SET HIS SPIRIT FREE…
IF HE COULD ONLY SEE WHAT I SEE

**DEREK.**
*(Under final chorus.)*
TWO DIFFERENT WORLDS
TIRED OF BEIN' DOWN, SICK OF BEIN' POOR
NOBODY EVER REALLY GAVE ME A PRAYER
YOU'RE LOOKIN' OUT FOR ME-I THINK YOU REALLY
    CARE
THIS COULD BE MY ONE SHOT-MAYBE ALL I GOT
I DON'T WANNA DIE; I WANNA BE FREE
IT'S NOT TOO LATE FOR ME
MAYBE I CAN TRY AND SEE…WHAT YOU SEE

**TEACHER.**
IF YOU COULD SEE WHAT I SEE.

**DEREK.**
I WANNA SEE WHAT YOU SEE.

**TEACHER.**
IF YOU COULD SEE WHAT I SEE.

**DEREK.**
I WANNA SEE WHAT YOU SEE.

**TEACHER.**
THEN SEE IT.

*(Others ENTER & stand in doorway & observe the last part of the song. JAKE Steps between TEACHER & DEREK to lighten the mood with a "Lion King" reference.)*

**JAKE.** Hakuna Matata, Timon and Pumba! Thank you. Thank you very much! My work here is done! *(All laugh/react to JAKE'S joke. He succeeds in breaking the tension.)*
**TEACHER.** *(Sincere to DEREK.)* Start with your real friends…these guys see you and love you for who you are…look them in the eye and be the man you dreamed you'd be.
**DEREK.** You mean "Ballet Guy"?
**TEACHER.** *(Smiles)* Maybe. I think you know what I mean.
**DEREK.** I think I do.
**SKYE.** Man, we are all just poster children for the Dr. Phil Show.
**ANGEL.** *(Referring to JANE.)* Except for Susie Smileyface here. Apparently she has no problems at all.
**JANE.** What? I have problems.
**ANGEL.** Feel free to share.
**JANE.** My Biggest problem…MY BIGGEST PROBLEM is that *(Sincere)* I don't seem to have any…
**DEREK.** Told ya.
**AMY.** How's that a problem?
**JAKE.** And that's a problem, why?
**JANE.** *(Calm & sincere.)* My biggest problem is that everyone teases me because I'm so happy. *(Mimicking)* "Ohhh, look at Miss Happy Pants." "Miss Smiley — she's so fake. Nobody can be *that* happy. *(Sincere)* Well I am! I *choose* to be happy and I see that as a good thing. Isn't that ultimately what everybody wants? So there's my big ugly secret. *(Long pause.)* Look, everybody has problems. I

take care of my Mom who's fighting cancer, my dad works all the time and my 4 year old brother, Ben thinks he's a dog. *(Others laugh.)* No, really he thinks he's a dog. *(Others laugh.)* Really. *(Others get quiet - totally believing her.)* Psych! *(JANE Laughs.)* So, I have stuff to deal with and sometimes it gets me down. But the truth is, I have a pretty good life. Our parents love us and my mom is the most courageous person I've ever met. I certainly don't mind helping her. Besides, that's what families do...take care of each other. My mom taught me that life is what I choose to make it...I choose to be happy...and, if I ever get down. I just think of little Ben eating macaroni & cheese out of a dog bowl.

### #9 Sound Cue: *"PLAIN JANE"*

**JANE.**
I GUESS I LIKE TO GO BY MY OWN SET OF RULES
I CONCENTRATE ON WHAT I CAN CONTROL
I DON'T SPEND TIME OBSESSING OVER WAYS I CAN BE
    COOL
I JUST THINK ABOUT THE THINGS THAT FEED MY SOUL
NOW TAKE MY WORD, MY LIFE IS NOT AS PERFECT AS
    YOU THINK
BUT I CAN TURN MY STRAW TO GOLD WITH JUST A SIM-
PLE BLINK


THEY CALL ME "PLAIN JANE," CAUSE I MAKE GOOD
    GRADES AND RE-CHANNEL MY PAIN
I TRY TO SEE THE GOOD IN ALL PEOPLE AND THINGS,
BUT I'M MORE THAN WHAT I SEEM
YES, I LOOK ON THE BRIGHT SIDE – MY GLASS IS HALF
    FULL
I'M IN TOUCH WITH MYSELF, WHETHER HOME OR AT
    SCHOOL
SO IF TAKING THE BEST AND MAKING THE MOST OF MY
    LIFE MEANS I'M PLAIN...
THEN I'LL BE "PLAIN JANE"
JUST CALL ME "PLAIN JANE"

*(Dialogue [Over music]:)*

**AMY.** So how do you stay so positive all the time?

**JANE.** Nobody has it easy, but we all cope in our own way. My mom can't even get out of bed, so I take care of her while you guys are out partying or at the game. My mom & I are really close. I wouldn't trade a minute of the time I spend with her.

**ANGEL.** Must be nice.

**SKYE.** Really.

**JANE.** See, that's what I mean!  Everyone has good and bad aspects of their lives — it's what you choose to focus on that can make or break you.

**JAKE.** But seeing the bad always seems easier!

**JANE.** Maybe. So you look more closely.

**AMY.** Amen!  Life is too short for dwelling in negativity.

**LUKE.** Hey I feel where you're coming from — we're listening.

 

**JANE.**
SO THOUGH I CAN'T CHANGE EVERYTHING, I CAN SURE-
LY CHANGE MY MIND...
ASK WHAT CAN I BE GRATEFUL FOR TODAY?
I CAN'T MANIPULATE THE LANDSCAPE, BUT I CAN SEE
WITH BRAND NEW EYES,
ALWAYS BELIEVING FAITH AND LOVE WILL GUIDE MY
WAY
NOTHING IN THIS WORLD IS QUITE AS HOPELESS AS WE
THINK

 

**ALL.**
AND WE CAN TURN THIS STRAW TO GOLD WITH JUST A
SIMPLE BLINK!

 

**JANE.**
THEY CALL ME "PLAIN JANE," — I CHOOSE TO BE HAPPY
AND GET STUCK WITH THAT NAME
I TRY TO SEE THE GOOD IN ALL PEOPLE AND THINGS,
BUT I'M MORE THAN WHAT I SEEM

 

**ALL.**
YES, SHE LOOKS ON THE BRIGHT SIDE – HER GLASS IS

HALF FULL
SHE'S IN TOUCH WITH HERSELF, WHETHER HOME OR AT
    SCHOOL

JANE.
SO IF TAKING THE BEST AND MAKING THE MOST OF MY
    LIFE MEANS I'M PLAIN…
THEN CALL ME "PLAIN JANE"
GLAD TO BE "PLAIN JANE"
IT'S NICE TO MEET YOU…I'M "PLAIN JANE"
AND WHAT A RELIEF TO BE "PLAIN JANE"

**TEACHER.** Jane…I think you hit on something.

**JANE.** *(Surprised)* I did? What? What did I hit on?

**TEACHER.** It's not what happens in your life that matters most, it's how you react to it.

**DEREK.** Alright. *(Getting the 'big picture'.)* And…we've all got some common ground, right?

**JAKE.** Hey, I never wanted to be "Ballet Guy". *(SKYE swats him playfully.)*

**ANGEL.** Yeah, we've all got common ground,  but we don't always see that.

**SKYE.** Sometimes you gotta look for it.

**JANE.** You have to choose to see it.

**AMY.** Choose to look for it.

**JAKE.** To look beyond the football. *(All laugh.)*

**LUKE.**  Choose to make a difference.

**ANGEL.** Choose to look beneath the surface.

**TEACHER.**  Then, you'll really see.

**JANE.** That's it! I know what we can do for our project!

**ALL.** *(Excited)* We got it! We can do it. We're all over this project. *(Ad libs — jumping, high fives, arms around each other. They freeze in tableaux.)*

**TEACHER.** *(To audience.)*  Well, they completed their project and learned a lot about life.  I never had a doubt.

**#10 Sound Cue:**
***"UNDERSCORING — INTRODUCTION OF
PRESENTATION"***

*(Music changes — TEACHER walks briskly to center stage to address the assembly. Students break freeze & walk into formation for presentation.*
*SR to SL, JANE, JAKE, DEREK, AMY, LUKE, SKYE, ANGEL.)*

**TEACHER.** And now, ladies and gentlemen please welcome your classmates as they present "Project Reconnect"!

*(Each of their lines has significant, personal meaning. They truly understand each other and their connection is obvious.)*

**JANE.** *(To audience.)* During the preparation for this project, we discovered that…
**JAKE.** There are endless possibilities.
**DEREK.** We do have the power to create our own future.
**AMY.** The choices we make now can affect us forever.
**LUKE.** Think for yourself….follow *your* dreams.
**SKYE.** It's not okay to suffer. You can ask for help.
**ANGEL.** It's possible to learn from mistakes *other* people make and break the chain.
**JANE.** Happiness is all about attitude. Choose happiness.

*(The following lines are run together to create one smooth sentence.)*

**JANE.** Everyone…
**JAKE.** …has value…
**DEREK.** …sometimes…
**AMY.** …you need to…
**LUKE.** …look beneath…
**SKYE.** …the surface…
**ANGEL.** …to realize that.

### #11 Sound Cue: *"CAN U DIG IT? (FINALE)"*

*(Finale — this song IS their presentation for the school assembly.)*

**ALL.**
CAN U DIG IT? CAN U DIG IT?
CAN U DIG IT? CAN U DIG IT?

(CAN U DIG IT, COME ON)
CAN U DIG IT?  CAN U DIG IT?
CAN U DIG IT?  CAN U DIG IT?
(CAN U DIG IT)

   **LUKE.**
ALL OF US HAVE CHOICES — WE DON'T HAVE TWO BE
   ALONE

   **GUYS.**
THAT'S A FACT, SO HOLLA BACK, YO

   **ANGEL.**
JUST LOOK AT HOW MUCH WE HAVE GROWN.

   **DEREK.**
HAVE FAITH IN YOURSELF
TAKE THE TIME TO RELATE TO SOMEBODY ELSE
U AIN'T GOTTA TALK; TRY & LISTEN

   **JAKE.**
LISTEN, UP
CUZ U MIGHT BE MISSIN' THE GOOD STUFF
UNDER THE BOLD REBEL'S A WHOLE NEW LEVEL

   **GIRLS.**
LIVE EACH MOMENT LIKE IT'S YOUR LAST

   **ALL.**
CAN U DIG IT?  CAN U DIG IT?
CAN U DIG IT?  CAN U DIG IT?
(CAN U DIG IT, COME ON)
CAN U DIG IT?  CAN U DIG IT?
CAN U DIG IT?  CAN U DIG IT?
(CAN U DIG IT)

   **GUYS.**
RAISE THE ROOF
RAISE THE ROOF

RAISE THE ROOF
RAISE THE ROOF

**ALL.** *(Spoken)* Open your eyes and let this in. Every soul in this room is a possible friend.

**LUKE.**
STAND UP WHEN U FEEL THE POWER (REPEAT 3 TIMES)

**JAKE.**
STAND UP WHEN U FEEL THE POWER (REPEAT 2 TIMES)

**JANE.**
STAND UP WHEN U FEEL THE POWER

**ALL.**
STAND UP; CAN U FEEL THE POWER (NOW?)

*(Fugue section.)*

**PART 1 (JAKE & JANE).**
CAN U DIG IT?  CAN U DIG IT?
CAN U DIG IT?  CAN U DIG IT?
CAN U DIG IT?  CAN U DIG IT?
CAN U DIG IT?  CAN U DIG IT?
*(Repeat all twice.)*

**PART 2 (LUKE & DEREK).**
DON'T FIGHT IT; CAN'T DENY IT
MIGHT BE SURPRISED IF U TRY IT
SOME HIDE IT, GET SHORT-SIGHTED
MIGHT BE SURPRISED IF U TRY IT (REPEAT ALL 3 TIMES)

**PART 3 (ANGEL).**
THERE'S MORE 2 ME THAN WHAT U SEE
DITCH THE LABELS & SET YOUR MIND FREE (REPEAT)

**PART 4 (LUKE).**
ALL OF US HAVE CHOICES-WE DON'T HAVE 2 BE ALONE

THAT'S A FACT SO....HOLLA BACK, YO
JUST LOOK AT HOW MUCH WE HAVE GROWN

   **ALL.**
CAN U DIG IT?
THERE'S A TIE THAT BINDS US WITH LOVE!

    **#12 Sound Cue:** *"CURTAIN CALL"*


    THE END

# PROPERTY LIST

**General**
> Assorted trash cans, metal containers, soda can, a broom, etc. to use to create music during the Stomp-rhythm piece.
> Various book bags, purses, cell phones, ipods etc. as needed.

**Jane**
> Journal, "The List" (This book may be decorated in a kid-like fashion)

**Teacher**
> Drum sticks (to use as 'light-sabers')
> Football
> Books
> Notebook
> Pen
> Coffee cup

# COSTUME SUGGESTIONS

*All costumes should be contemporary street clothes that would be seen in a typical high school.*

JAKE.  Jeans & a sports jersey, baseball cap.

DEREK.  Tough & street-wise with a legitimate 'gangsta' look. Add jewelry, a do rag, hat, sun glasses etc.

AMY.  Should be trendy, upscale, feminine and fully accessorized.

ANGEL.  Dressed in dark colors, should look harsh, rough and give the appearance that she is 'drugged-out'.

LUKE.  Nice, casual, upscale clothes yet NOT preppy. He comes from a  wealthy family, but he is a laid back, down-to-earth kind of guy.

SKYE. Dresses in an artsy, colorful, layered look with an edge.

JANE.  Simple, comfortable clothes in earth tones, with a splash of a bright color such as yellow and perhaps a fun hat.  Eye glasses.

TEACHER.  Should be dressed in fun, contemporary clothes.  She is a teacher that definitely has the 'cool-factor' while maintaining a professional appearance.

# SET SUGGESTION

BENEATH THE SURFACE takes place in a unique, high school classroom. The décor represents a variety of art, pop-culture, philosophy, music, sports & current events. The walls are covered in posters, meaningful quotes, artwork, news clippings, a bulletin board etc. There are 7 chairs or 7 student desks and one larger desk & chair for the teacher. They are not lined up in a traditional fashion. There could be a sitting/reading area in the corner, filled with pillows.

**Suggestions for a mobile set with easy storage for touring productions:**

3 free-standing accordion flats. Each of these flats is designed with 4 panels, attached with hinges so that they fold up for storage and expand into a zigzag formation to become freestanding flats. They remain on stage the entire show. The flats are painted to look like brick walls OR pre-made faux brick plywood may be used. Wall decorations include posters, quotes, art, bulletin board, newspaper articles etc.

**Placement of set pieces:**

1 accordion flat stage right, 1 accordion flat stage left and 1 accordion flat upstage center of the other two, thus creating two entrances upstage center.

Teacher's desk & chair, upstage left. Large, metal trash can beside desk. Pen holder, bookends with several books, notebook, coffee cup, drum sticks etc. on desk.

Student's chairs placed in an unconventional formation in the room. The characters may move the chairs at various times throughout the show.

Push broom leaning up against the wall stage right.